FOUR DOLLARS
AND FIFTY CENTS

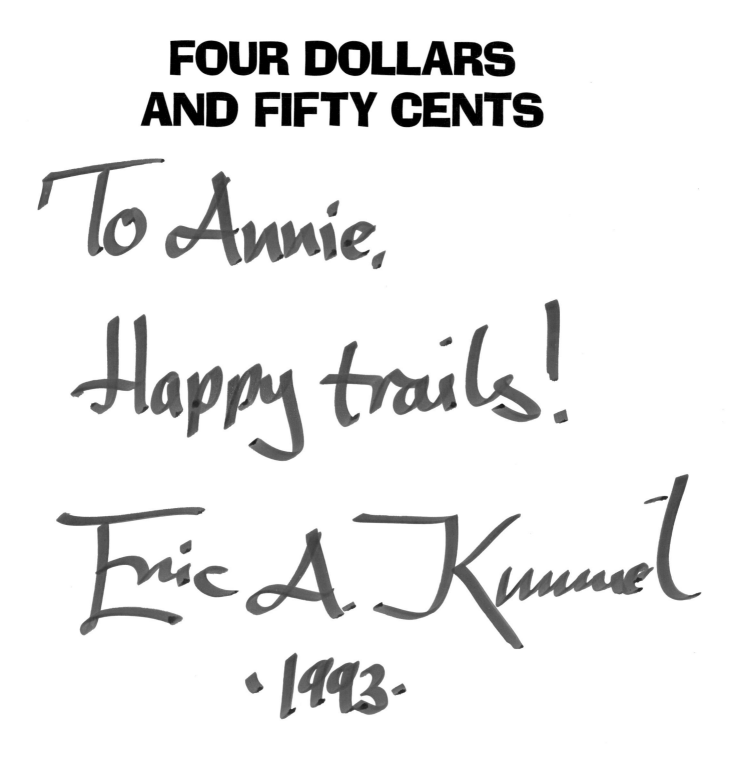

To Annie,

Happy trails!

Eric A. Kimmel

· 1993 ·

For Marianne

FOUR DOLLARS
AND FIFTY CENTS

by Eric A. Kimmel

illustrated by Glen Rounds

Holiday House / New York

It's a terrible thing to call a cowboy a deadbeat, but in Shorty Long's case it was true. He owed everybody money, from Big Oscar the blacksmith to Widow Macrae, who ran the Silver Dollar Cafe and baked the best biscuits west of the Rockies.

"Shorty ain't a bad sort. He just hates to pay for anything he thinks he can get free," Big Oscar told the widow one afternoon over coffee at the Silver Dollar.

The widow brought Oscar another plate of biscuits. "How am I gonna keep this place going if folks won't pay their bills? Shorty's the worst. He owes me four dollars and fifty cents."

Big Oscar shook his head. "You got as much chance of collecting that money as seeing Custer ride back from the Little Bighorn."

Widow Macrae picked up her rolling pin. "That's what you think. I'm driving out to the Circle K this afternoon. If Shorty won't pay what he owes, I'll lay him out flatter 'n the bottom of a skillet."

As soon as Oscar left, Widow Macrae hitched her two horses, Clementine and Evangeline, to the buckboard and drove out to the Circle K ranch. Duck Pooley saw her coming. He rode back to the corral to warn Shorty.

"Widow Macrae's coming! She's got a rolling pin in her hand and an awful mean look in her eye. You better come up with that money, Shorty."

"Boys, you gotta help me!" Shorty yelped.

"Why don't you just pay what you owe?"

"It ain't that simple. If I paid the widow back, everybody I owe money to'd expect the same. I'd end up broker 'n a mess of eggs."

The Circle K boys decided to help Shorty out just for the fun of seeing what would happen. They knocked together a few boards to make a coffin. When Widow Macrae drove up, she found Shorty lying in it. He looked real peaceful. The Circle K boys stood around blubbering, wiping their noses on their sleeves.

Widow Macrae got down from the buckboard. ''What happened to Shorty?'' she asked.

"He's gone to the last roundup," the Circle K boys told her. "A bronco threw him. He landed on his head."

The widow leaned over for a closer look. Shorty looked deader 'n a Christmas tree in August. But she still wasn't sold, although she kept her suspicions to herself.

"Poor Shorty. It hurts my heart to see him like this. Where do you boys figure on burying him?"

"Why, here on the ranch. Somewheres."

Widow Macrae frowned. "That's not right. Shorty deserves better than sagebrush and coyotes. I know you don't have time to spare, what with the spring roundup coming on. But if you let me take Shorty back to town, I'll see he gets a decent burial."

The Circle K boys could hardly refuse.

"Then it's settled. Some of you boys load Shorty onto the buckboard. Try not to bounce him around too much."

"I'll nail the lid down," Duck Pooley volunteered.

"Not just yet," said Widow Macrae. "I want to see him one last time before I put him in the ground. Shorty Long was my friend."

That sure was news to Shorty. He didn't say a word, but he was thinking hard, mostly about what he'd like to do to Duck Pooley.

With the coffin loaded, Widow Macrae headed back towards town. She turned off onto the Boot Hill road. Boot Hill is where they bury cowboys like Shorty, who die with their boots on. It's a mighty rough road for a feller's last journey.

Widow Macrae reined in at the top of the hill next to a freshly dug grave. She got down from the buckboard, unhitched the horses, and turned them loose to graze. Then she took hold of the coffin and dragged it out of the wagon. Shorty saw stars when the coffin hit the ground, but he was bound and determined not to pay that four dollars and fifty cents, so he lay still.

The widow studied him hard. "Can you hear me, Shorty? If you can, listen good. I don't know if you're dead or not, but I'm gonna keep my eyes on you all night. If you ain't moved by morning, into the ground you go!"

Poor Shorty! It was pay up or be buried alive—and he couldn't make up his mind which was worse! The sun went down. With Widow Macrae's eyes fixed on him tight, Shorty lay still in his coffin, not moving a muscle, not hardly breathing, waiting for something to happen.

On about midnight something did. Riders! He heard them coming up the Boot Hill road. Widow Macrae ducked behind a tombstone. As for Shorty, he was sure it was a posse of dead cowboys riding back from the grave for one last roundup. He lay in his coffin, stiff as rawhide, hoping that with all the graves up there they wouldn't notice one extra corpse.

Three riders reined in at the top of Boot Hill. They got off their horses. One lit a lantern while the other two lugged an iron strongbox over to the open grave. Anyone would recognize them at once. It was Big Nose George Parrott and two of his gang, Smiley Dunlap and the Oregon Kid. The outlaws started bragging about a train they robbed that afternoon. They came to the graveyard to divide the loot. No one would think of looking for outlaws on Boot Hill. Not live ones, anyway.

Shorty was in a heap of trouble. If those outlaws caught him spying on them, he wouldn't have to worry about being a fake corpse. Big Nose George drew his six-gun.

"Stand back, boys! I'll settle this business!"

He fired a shot into the strongbox padlock. Shorty nearly gave up the ghost. He thought that bullet was meant for him.

"Yahoo! We struck it rich!"

The Oregon Kid kicked open the lid. He and Smiley reached inside and began throwing fistfuls of hundred dollar bills into the air. That made Big Nose George real mad.

"Quit that clowning! This ain't the circus! You boys pick up them greenbacks and put 'em back where you found 'em!"

"Aw, George!"

"Aw, George nothing! We're gonna divvy it up business-like. No grabbing!"

The Kid and Smiley started picking up the money. One of the bills landed in Shorty's coffin.

''Holy Hannah! What's this? There's a dead 'un here!''

"Don't drop your britches, boys. Dead 'uns don't bite."
Big Nose George moseyed over for a closer look. "Why, it's
some poor cowpoke whose burying had to wait till morning.
They should've covered him up, though. It ain't decent leav-
ing a feller out in the open where the buzzards can get at him.
But that ain't none of our concern. Bring over them bills and
let's get started."

"Can't we close that coffin first?" the Kid asked. "Dead 'uns give me the willies."

"Sure, go ahead," said Big Nose George.

The Kid slammed the coffin lid right down on Shorty's nose! Tears came to Shorty's eyes. He clenched his teeth to keep from yelling.

"What's the matter?" Smiley asked.

"This lid don't fit."

"Let me try." Smiley sat down hard on the coffin. He packed a lot of weight. The lid mashed Shorty's nose into his face. Shorty saw stars, but not the ones in the sky.

"What's keeping you two?" Big Nose George growled.

"This lid won't lay flat."

"Let me see." Big Nose George had a look. "Are you both crack-brained? Use your eyes. This feller's nose sticks up a mile. It's way too long for the coffin."

"What'll we do?"

"Easy! He don't need a sniffer where he's going. I'll cut it off with my bowie knife!"

That was enough for Shorty. He sat up in his coffin and hollered, "Hold on, boys! I ain't that dead!"

Big Nose George nearly dropped his teeth.

Smiley let out a yell as the whole gang ran for their horses.

Those outlaws shot out of that graveyard faster than fireworks!

Widow Macrae laughed fit to bust. When she was all laughed out, she came from behind the tombstone and gave Shorty the scolding of his life.

"I hope you learned your lesson. You nearly got your nose cut off for four dollars and fifty cents!"

Shorty was too embarrassed to say anything. He and Widow Macrae gathered up the money the outlaws left behind. In the morning they took it to the railroad agent in town. He gave them a five-hundred-dollar reward to divide between them.

Shorty rubbed his nose. "I reckon we're even now."

"Not quite," said Widow Macrae. "You still owe me four dollars and fifty cents."

Shorty stared glumly at his pile of fifty-dollar bills. "I don't have no change. How about if I come by tomorrow and settle up?"

"I'll expect you," Widow Macrae said.

But so far as anyone knows, he hasn't paid her yet.

This story first appeared in *Cricket, The Magazine for Children*

Library of Congess Cataloging-in-Publication Data
Kimmel, Eric A.
Four dollars and fifty cents / written by Eric A. Kimmel :
illustrated by Glen Rounds.—1st ed.
p.   cm.
Summary: To avoid paying the Widow Macrae the four dollars
and fifty cents he owes her, deadbeat cowboy Shorty Long
plays dead and almost gets buried alive.
ISBN 0-8234-0817-5
[1. Cowboys—Fiction.   2. West (U.S.)—Fiction.
3. Humorous stories.]   I. Rounds, Glen, ill.   II. Title.
PZ7.K5648Fo   1990   [E]—dc20   89-77515   CIP   AC